Mine!

A Sesame Street Book About Sharing

Featuring Jim Henson's Sesame Street Muppets

By Linda Hayward • Illustrated by Norman Gorbaty
Random House/Children's Television Workshop

Library of Congress Cataloging-in-Publication Data:
Hayward, Linda. Mine! : A Sesame Street book about sharing. (A Just right book) SUMMARY: After fighting over their toys, Little Bert and Little Ernie discover the advantages of sharing. [1. Sharing—Fiction. 2. Puppets—Fiction] I. Gorbaty, Norman, ill. II. Children's Television Workshop. III. Title. IV. Series: Just right book (New York, N.Y.) PZ7.H31495Mi 1988 [E] 87-42810 ISBN: 0-394-89599-1

Manufactured in Singapore   6 7 8 9 0
JUST RIGHT BOOKS is a trademark of Random House, Inc.

One day Little Ernie was playing on Sesame Street. He wanted to ride in the big red wagon.

"Go! Go!" said Little Ernie, and he bounced back and forth in the wagon. But the big red wagon would not go.

So Little Ernie played with his fire
truck instead.

"Wheee-eee!" went Little Ernie as he
pushed his fire truck.

Round and round went the wheels.
Clang-clang went the bell.
Little Bert came over. He wanted to
push the fire truck too.

"No!" said Little Ernie. "Mine!"

Little Bert sat down in the big red wagon. He wanted to ride.

He sat and sat and waited and waited. But the big red wagon would not go.

So Little Bert played with his pull-along pigeon instead.

"Peep-peep!" went Little Bert as he pulled along his pull-along pigeon.

Wobble, wobble went the pigeon.
Clack-clack went the wheels.
Little Ernie came over. He wanted to
pull the toy pigeon too.

"No!" said Little Bert. "Mine!"

Little Ernie picked up his toy telephone and pushed three buttons. One, two, three! Ring, ring, ring!

Little Bert picked up his toy telephone and pushed three buttons. Four, five, six! Ring, ring, ring!

"Hello? Hello? Hello?" shouted Little Ernie.

"Hello?" Little Bert shouted back.

"Who is this?" asked Little Ernie.

"Bert," said Little Bert. "Who is this?"

"Ernie," said Little Ernie. "Can you play?"

"Yes," said Little Bert. "Can you?"

"Yes," said Little Ernie. "Bye-bye!"

"Bye-bye!" said Little Bert.

Little Ernie climbed into the big red wagon. Little Bert began to pull. He pulled Little Ernie up and down Sesame Street.

Round and round went the wheels.
"Wheee-eee!" cried Little Ernie.
"Here comes the fire truck!" said Little Bert.

Then it was Little Bert's turn to ride.
He climbed into the big red wagon.
Little Ernie began to push. He pushed
Little Bert up and down Sesame Street.

Round and round went the wheels.
"Here comes the fire truck!" cried
Little Ernie.
"Clang-clang!" said Little Bert.

Up and down and around and around
went Little Bert and Little Ernie.
They shared the big red wagon.

Then it was time for a snack.

Little Ernie and Little Bert saw a nice juicy apple.

"Mine!" said Little Ernie.

"Mine!" said Little Bert.

They shared the apple too.
Little Ernie ate half an apple.
And so did Little Bert.